THE
PIRATE
PRINCESS

AND OTHER FAIRY TALES

THE PIRATE PRINCESS

AND OTHER FAIRY TALES

BY

NEIL PHILIP

ILLUSTRATED BY

MARK WEBER

ARTHUR A. LEVINE BOOKS
AN IMPRINT OF SCHOLASTIC INC.

Thanks to Professor Shaul Magid of Indiana University
for his expert commentary on the introduction and notes.

LIBRARY OF CONGRESS CATALOGING-IN-PUBLICATION DATA

Philip, Neil. The pirate princess and other fairy tales /

by Neil Philip; illustrated by Mark Weber. — 1st American ed. p. cm.

Includes bibliographical references (p.). 1. Legends, Jewish. 2. Fairy tales. I. Weber, Mark (Mark A.),

1958- ill. II. Nachman, of Bratslav, 1772-1810. Selections. III. Title.

BM530.P48 2005   398.2'089'924—dc22   2004016949

ISBN 0-590-10855-7

10 9 8 7 6 5 4 3 2   05 06 07 08 09

Printed in Singapore   46

First edition, October 2005

The type was set in 13.5 Bembo.

The artwork was created in gouache.

For Susan, Barry, and Julian with love

– N. P.

For Chris, Kelsie, and Mom, with love and smiles

– M.W.

CONT

ENTS

INTRODUCTION

Rabbi nahman ben simha of bratslav (1772-1810) is still revered today as an important religious teacher. He was also a great storyteller, whose fairy tales, composed at the same time as the Grimms started collecting their German folktales, are both as personal and as universal as those of Hans Christian Andersen.

Nahman was born in Medzhibozh in Ukraine, which was also the birthplace of the mystical Jewish movement of Hasidism, founded by Nahman's great-grandfather Israel Ba'al Shem Tov. Hasidism is a movement that seeks personal redemption and communion with God through study, prayer, dance, and storytelling. It is structured in all-male schools or courts, each centered on a charismatic spiritual leader known as a zaddik (righteous man) or a rebbe (teacher or master). Nahman was destined from birth to be such a man.

Rabbi Nahman believed he was the fifth and last in a series of great religious leaders of the Jews: Moses, Simeon ben Yohai, Isaac Luria, the Ba'al Shem Tov, and finally himself. In 1806, Nahman told his disciples that the Messiah would arrive within a few years, and that he knew "the precise year, month, and day on which he was expected." But his plans were shattered

when his infant son Shlomo Ephraim, on whom his messianic hopes were pinned, died from an unknown illness.

This tragedy threw Nahman into crisis. Although his key teaching was "Never despair," he now came close to the brink. He saved himself through storytelling. In his beautiful and complex fairy tales, he consoled himself and his disciples with dreams of the coming redemption.

In the summer of 1806, Rabbi Nahman announced, "The time has come for me to begin telling stories." Until his death in Uman in 1810 from tuberculosis — a disease that wracked his final years and perhaps contributed something to the feverish intensity of his imagination — the fairy tale became the principal focus of his religious teaching. He believed passionately in the power of story-telling to change the world, saying, "If one is to believe what people say, stories are written to put them to sleep. I tell mine to wake them up."

Nahman created only thirteen new fairy tales, rich in mystical and folkloric meaning. Four appear in this book: "The Pirate Princess," "The Gem Prince," "The Merchant and the Poor Man," and "The Lost Princess." He also told a number of short parables and folktales, such as "The Fixer," "The Treasure," and "The Turkey Prince."

The commentator David G. Roskies points out that the fairy tales, which Nahman told in idiomatic colloquial Yiddish, were intended for various audiences who would understand them on multiple levels. They can be understood as deliberately skewed variations of traditional folktales, as religious allegories, as symbolic reenactments of Kabbalistic mythology,

and as masked autobiography. A few of these interpretations and connections are offered in the notes on each story.

It is as well to admit straightforwardly that there is a profound element of Nahman's storytelling that cannot be captured in any retelling. No one outside the Hasidic and Kabbalistic traditions could hope to understand the subtle nuances of mystical meaning hidden in the intricate folds of Nahman's tales — and these subtlest meanings are the very ones which mere translation tends to obliterate. To add to that the simplification and reexpression that the stories have undergone at my hands in adapting them for a general readership is to admit that Rabbi Nahman's mystical teachings must be either corrupted or lost in the process.

However, there is another inner secret to the stories that I hope can survive. That is the secret that binds Nahman's tales not to the hidden traditions of the Kabbalah, but to the open traditions of worldwide storytelling. To recognize that Rabbi Nahman's fairy tales have deep roots both in the Yiddish and Slavic folktale traditions and in oriental story-cycles is not to deny him his originality. It was Nahman's belief that in the original cataclysm of creation, all the elements of the true and eternal story of redemption were scattered through the world, to be pieced haphazardly together in the form of fairy tales. "In the tales which other people tell," he said, "there are many secrets and lofty matters, but the tales have been ruined in that they are lacking much. They are confused and not told in the proper sequence: What belongs at the beginning they tell at the end and vice versa."

Nahman's recognition of the way in which traditional fairy tales are constructed from the building blocks of story motifs predates that of folklorists by several generations; the Grimms would not even publish the first edition of their pioneering collection of German fairy tales until 1812. But Nahman was not trying to collect or preserve such tales. He understood his retellings as acts of tikkun — repair and restoration of a broken world. So it is always meaningful when Nahman's tales veer, as they do, from the expected folktale pattern.

One of the great pleasures of reading Rabbi Nahman's tales is to enjoy the beautiful play of his mind as he takes apart the traditional fairy tale and reassembles it into something new and wonderful. Nahman responded to the deep structure of the traditional tale with a unique creative passion.

The fairy tales of Rabbi Nahman are, wrote Elie Wiesel in *Souls on Fire,* "among the most spellbinding in Hasidic literature. They constitute a universe of their own in which dreamers go beyond their dreams, beyond their desires, swept away by their quest for imagination and salvation and an infinite craving for innocence and wonder."

It perhaps tells us all we need to know about the centrality of these fairy tales to Rabbi Nahman's vision of the world to learn that, in a play on the wording of the original Hebrew, he interpreted God's resolution in Genesis 1:26 not as "Let us make man in our own image," but "Let us make man with an imagination."

THE PIRATE PRINCESS

THERE WERE ONCE an emperor and a king who were both perfectly happy, except for one thing: They both longed to have a child. So they each set off around the world, searching for a cure for their childlessness. Traveling from opposite directions, they met at last at the same inn.

Although they had never met before, one ruler can always recognize another. Soon they had admitted who they were and the reason for their quest.

"If neither of us has found a cure," said the emperor, "then we must simply put our trust in God." And the king agreed.

They made a pact that if, when they reached their homes, one had a boy and the other a girl, the two children should be married.

When the emperor returned home, he fathered a daughter. When the king returned home, he fathered a son. But in all the excitement, the pact they had made was quite forgotten.

When the time came, the emperor sent his daughter to the finest tutor in the world, and the king sent his son to the same tutor. The young man and woman fell in love and vowed to marry. The king's son took a ring and placed it on the finger of the emperor's daughter — so they were married in the sight of God.

Then their fathers summoned them home, and they had to part.

Many suitors asked for the hand of the princess, but she refused them all, for she had already given her heart. She pined for the king's son, and he for her. The emperor tried hard to please his daughter, but he could not make her happy.

As for the prince, he missed her so much that he made himself ill. But when people asked him what the matter was, he would not tell them. So then they asked his servant, who had been with him at the tutor's, and the servant told them everything.

The king then remembered the pact he had made with the emperor so long ago. He wrote to the emperor reminding him of their agreement, and suggesting that the wedding should go ahead.

The emperor was no longer enthusiastic about the match, but he did not want to break his word. He wrote, "Send your son to me, and I will test him. If I find him worthy to rule the kingdom, he shall marry my daughter."

When the prince arrived, he asked to see the emperor's daughter, but the emperor said, "Later, when you have proved your worth." The emperor showed him into a room full of documents and said, "First, I would be obliged if you would attend to a few trifling matters of business for me."

The documents were to do with the affairs of state, and as soon as the prince had dealt with one of them, two more arrived. He realized that he would never be finished, and therefore would never see his sweetheart.

Then one day, as he walked through a hall on the way to his paperwork, he saw her reflection in a mirror. He was so overcome with love that he fainted.

She went over to him and revived him. "My true love!" she said. "I will never marry anyone but you."

"But what can we do?" he asked. "I can tell that your father will never let us marry."

"We will find a way," she replied.

They decided to run away together. They hired a ship and set out to sea.

When they had sailed far enough away, they put into a forested shore to rest. The princess took off her ring and gave it to the prince to hold while she lay down to sleep. The prince watched over her as she slept. When she woke, he put the ring down next to her and went to sleep himself.

When they were refreshed, they went back to the ship. Once they were aboard, they realized that they had forgotten the ring. She sent him back to look for it, but he could not find the place. He wandered round and round in the forest until he was completely lost.

When he did not come back, she returned to the forest to search for him, and soon she too was lost.

The prince blundered around until he came to a path that led him to a town. As he had no money, he had to work — but he was a king's son, and only knew how to order servants about. So he became a servant himself.

The princess walked in a circle until she came back to the sea. There she found the ring and hung it for safekeeping around her neck. But she could not find the prince. She decided to stay by the shore, living off the fruit that grew there and spending the day on the beach on the lookout for a ship. At night she would sleep in the branches of a tree to be safe from wild animals.

In another land, there was a rich merchant who traded all over the world. He had one son.

One day the son said to him, "You are getting old. You should let me help you. Because you never let me do anything, no one takes any notice of me, and when you die, I won't know how to run the business. Give me a ship full of merchandise, so I can learn how to trade."

His father gave him a ship full of merchandise as he asked, and he began to sail the seas, trading wherever he went. Soon he had sold all the original merchandise and filled the ship with new goods bought out of the profit he had made.

Scanning the sea one day, he saw reflected in its surface the image of a tree with a girl sitting in it. He called the sailors to come and look, and they too saw the tree and the girl. He decided to investigate.

He got into a rowboat and rowed across the sea, guided by the image. When he reached the shore, he found the princess sitting in the tree. "Who are you?" he asked.

"I will not tell you until we reach your home," she replied.

"All right," he said. "Come down." And he held up his arms to catch her.

"I will not come down unless you promise not to touch me until we reach your home."

"I promise," he said. "But when we get home, will you marry me?"

"Not until you introduce me to your father," she replied.

"That's fair," he said, so she went with him to the ship.

Soon he discovered that she could play beautiful music and speak many languages. He was amazed to have found such a wonderful girl.

When they reached his home port, he wanted to take her straight to his house, but she said, "You should go home first and tell your father and your family about me, so they can welcome me with honor."

He agreed.

Then she said, "While you are gone, you should allow the crew to celebrate. Give them wine so that they can drink to our health."

He went home to prepare his family and left the sailors to drink themselves into a stupor on the dockside. When the last one had fallen asleep, the princess unfurled the sails, raised the anchor, and took the ship out to sea.

When the young merchant arrived with his father and all his family to show off his new bride and his fine cargo, the ship was gone. He could only splutter, "It was here before, I swear!"

They woke up the drunken sailors, but none of them knew anything at all. The ship and its cargo had vanished.

The old merchant was so angry with his feckless son that he disinherited him, and drove him out of his house to live as a wandering beggar.

Meanwhile, the princess was sailing the seven seas. As she sailed, she passed close to a palace that a king had built right by the shore, to enjoy the sea breezes and watch the ships go by. The king looked out and saw what seemed to be a ship with no sailors and no passengers. He called his servants, and they could see the ship too, so they decided to investigate.

They rowed out to the ship, waving to the princess. The princess wanted to sail on, but they begged her to come back to the palace.

Now, this king had never married. Either the ladies he liked had not liked him, or vice versa. When he saw the beautiful princess, he knew she was the right woman for him. He asked her straight out, "Will you marry me?"

She answered, "You must swear not to ask my name or to touch me until we are legally married." And he swore.

Then she told him, "Also, you must leave my ship exactly as it is. Then everyone can see what riches I have brought to the marriage, and no one can say you have married a pauper." Again, he agreed.

He sent thick, embossed invitations to all the kings of the world, asking them to his wedding. In the meantime, he built the princess a palace of her own and gave her eleven young women, all daughters of lords, to wait on her.

One day, as the wedding approached, the princess suggested to her waiting women that they should spend the day on her ship. "We can have fun," she said.

When they were on the ship, the waiting women sang and danced until they were exhausted. Afterward, the princess gave them some of the same heady wine she had served to the sailors, and soon they were all fast asleep. Then she unfurled the sails, raised the anchor, and took the ship out to sea.

When the king saw that the ship was gone, he was very upset, for he had promised the princess that it would not be touched. He went to her palace to tell her the sad news, but she was gone, and her waiting women too.

When the eleven lords realized that their daughters had been abducted from under the king's nose, they were very angry. They deposed him and sent him into exile.

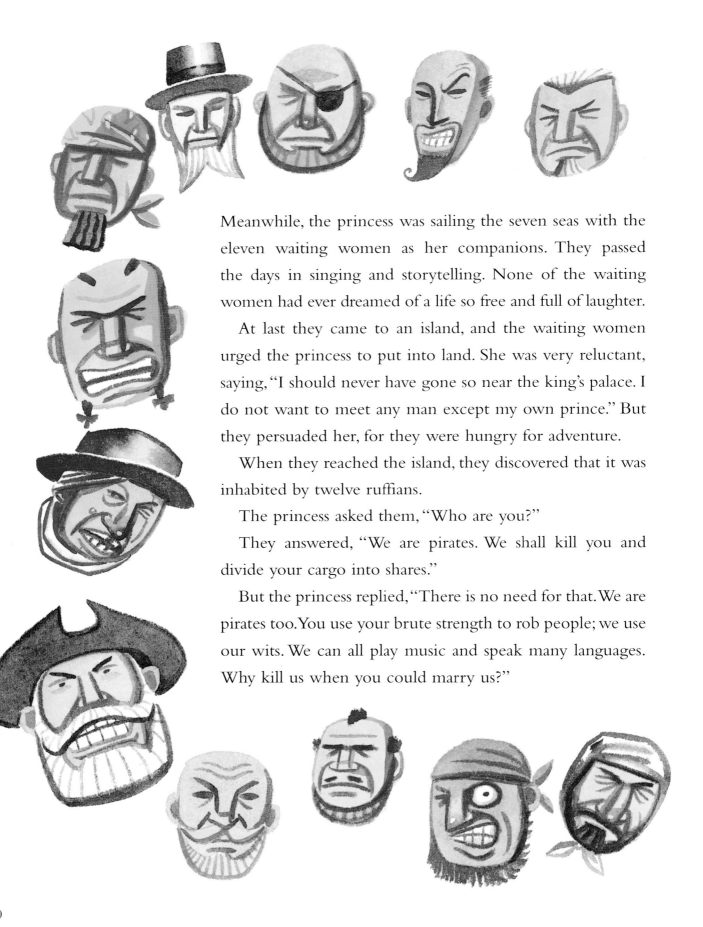

Meanwhile, the princess was sailing the seven seas with the eleven waiting women as her companions. They passed the days in singing and storytelling. None of the waiting women had ever dreamed of a life so free and full of laughter.

At last they came to an island, and the waiting women urged the princess to put into land. She was very reluctant, saying, "I should never have gone so near the king's palace. I do not want to meet any man except my own prince." But they persuaded her, for they were hungry for adventure.

When they reached the island, they discovered that it was inhabited by twelve ruffians.

The princess asked them, "Who are you?"

They answered, "We are pirates. We shall kill you and divide your cargo into shares."

But the princess replied, "There is no need for that. We are pirates too. You use your brute strength to rob people; we use our wits. We can all play music and speak many languages. Why kill us when you could marry us?"

The pirates agreed to that, and they also agreed not to ask the women's names or to touch them until they were married. Each pirate chose the woman he would marry the next day; the pirate chief chose the princess. Then the princess showed the pirates all the goods on the ship, and in return, the pirate chief showed her the secret cave where he had hidden his treasure.

That night, the princess offered the pirates some of the same strong wine she had given the sailors and the waiting women. They drank a toast to each of the twelve women in turn and became so drunk, they fell to the ground in a stupor. As they lay there snoring, the princess gave each woman a sack.

"While they are asleep, each woman must steal the treasure of the man who has dared to claim her," she said.

They fetched all the treasure from the pirates' secret hiding places and loaded it onto the ship. There were so many precious stones and so much gold that they had to throw most of the other cargo off the ship to make room for it.

Then the princess said, "In the future, let us dress like men. Then we will be safe from unwanted attention." So they each sewed themselves some men's clothing and set sail once more.

When they came to a big city, they decided to sail into port to buy supplies. Now that they were dressed in men's clothes, no one would recognize or bother them.

When they disembarked, they found all the people of the city standing around and looking up into the sky. So they stood and looked up too.

From the sky, a bird came spiraling down and settled on the head of the pirate princess.

A great roar went up from the crowd: "Long live the king!" And the princess was carried on the shoulders of the people to the palace. That was how the people of that city chose their king. When the old king died, they released a bird, which they called the Bird of Happiness, and whomever the bird alighted on became king.

When the princess had been crowned king, she announced that she wished to marry, and said that all her subjects should come to the city to attend her wedding. She had a well dug outside the city gates to refresh weary travelers and ordered that her portrait should be hung up by the well. Anyone who looked startled or upset when he saw the portrait should be arrested.

When they saw the portrait, most people just said, "So that is our new king." But there were three travelers, each footsore and road-weary, ragged and exhausted, who reacted with the same violent mixture of grief and joy when they saw the new king's face. These three were arrested and taken to the king.

They were her true love, the prince; the merchant's son, whose ship she had stolen; and the exiled king, who had wanted to marry her. None of them understood what was happening. Although they had reacted strongly to the portrait, they did not think it could be the princess — for she was dressed in men's clothes, and was a king.

She addressed the king first. "Do you not recognize me?" she said. "Once you wished to make me your queen. You showered me with gifts, but not with love. But you have suffered enough. Take the eleven waiting women home, the lords will forgive you, and you can be king again."

Then she turned to the merchant's son. "You too wished to marry me," she said. "To you, I was a prize, something to show off to your father. But you too have suffered enough. Your father turned you out because you

lost a ship full of cargo. Take it back — only now the cargo is all gold and jewels. Your father will forgive you."

And then she turned to the prince. "As for you, my love, your wanderings are over. We were separated once. We never shall be again."

She took the ring from around her neck, and the prince placed it on her finger. And they ruled the land together, in peace and wisdom.

THE
FIXER

THERE WAS ONCE a king who had everything. He ruled unchallenged, he could buy anything he fancied, and he had nothing to worry about. But still his mind was troubled. *Why am I not happy, when I have everything I want?* he wondered. *What is happiness? Can you buy it?*

So the king disguised himself as an ordinary person and walked out into the night to listen at doors and windows and hear what people were saying. All of them were pouring out their worries; not one was happy.

Then he came to a tumbledown house, so dilapidated that the windows had fallen off their hinges and the roof had caved in. Inside, the king at last saw a happy man. He was sitting on a pile of rubble, playing the fiddle and smiling. Before him was a plate of food and a bottle of wine. The sound of the man's fiddle was full of joy.

The king went into the house and greeted him. "Are you truly happy?" he asked.

"I'm as happy as a man in his right mind," the man replied. And he asked the king to share his plate of food and his bottle of wine. Afterward, the king wrapped himself in his cloak and settled down to sleep in the ruined house.

In the morning, the king asked the man, "How do you live?"

"I'm a fixer," he replied. "Things break, and people ask me to mend them. I don't make anything, but there's nothing I can't mend. And when I've mended enough things to buy myself some food and some drink, I come home and play my fiddle. Who could want for more?"

When the king heard this, he agreed it sounded like a carefree existence. There was no reason why the fixer should not be happy. But then he thought, *What if there were no broken things for him to mend? Would he still be happy then?* So when the king got back to the palace, he issued a decree that no one was to pay to have anything fixed. They must mend it themselves or buy new.

So that day when the fixer went out looking for work, there was none to be had. No one would disobey the king's decree. Things looked bad for the fixer, but he trusted in God, so he did not let himself become downhearted. "Something will turn up," he told himself.

On the way home, he saw a rich man chopping wood. "Surely a man of your standing doesn't have to chop his own wood?" said the fixer.

"I agree it's beneath me," said the rich man, "but I couldn't find anyone willing to do it for me. It's giving me blisters on my hands. Look!" The rich man held out his soft, pale hands, and the fixer saw that they were indeed growing red, for they had never done any hard work before.

"I'll do it for you," said the fixer. "My hands are already rough."

When the fixer had chopped the wood, the rich man paid him enough to buy himself food and drink. So the fixer went home quite happy.

That night, the king once more disguised himself as an ordinary man and went to eavesdrop on the people. Again, everyone was moaning and complaining, except for the fixer, who was sitting and playing his fiddle as happy as can be. The king went in and shared the fixer's supper as before.

"How did you earn the money for the food?" the king asked.

"Usually I fix things, as you know," said the fixer, "but the king has issued a decree against that, so yesterday I chopped wood until I had earned enough money to buy my supper."

The next day, the king issued a decree against anyone paying for wood to be chopped. So when the fixer went around offering his services, no one would employ him. However, on the way home, he saw a rich man cleaning out a stable.

"That looks hard," he said.

"Too hard for me," said the rich man, "but I couldn't find anyone willing to do it for me. It's making me filthy. Look!"

The fixer saw that the rich man's dainty fingernails were engrained with dirt, and his fine clothes were getting soiled and bedraggled.

"Let me do it," said the fixer. "A bit of dirt will do me no harm."

When he had cleaned out all the muck, the rich man paid him enough to buy himself food and drink. So the fixer went home quite happy.

Once more, the king came by and found the fixer perfectly content. "How did you earn your money today?" the king asked, and the fixer explained that as the king had outlawed wood-chopping, he had taken to cleaning stables.

The next day, the king issued a decree against anyone paying to have their stables cleaned. So when the fixer went out looking for work, there was none to be had.

The fixer was in a fix.

Passing by the king's palace, the fixer saw the guards standing outside and thought, *The king will never outlaw his own guards!* So he went to an officer and volunteered for service in the royal guard. But he would only join if he could be paid every day and allowed to go home every night.

So the fixer was given a uniform and a sword, and when he had put them

on he looked just like a proper soldier. He earned his day's pay and went home that night quite happy.

The king came by again, and when he learned what had happened, he instructed the officer that no one should be paid daily.

When the fixer went to collect his money for the day, the officer said he was sorry, but he could not disobey the king's decree. "Tomorrow is payday, so then I will pay you for two days, but today I cannot pay you at all."

On the way home, the fixer worked out a plan. He removed the metal blade of his sword and pawned it so that he would have money to buy food and drink. Then he cut a wooden blade and fixed it to the sword. From a distance, no one would be able to tell the difference, and once he had been paid for the two days' work, he would be able to buy back the metal blade and reattach it.

That evening, when the king came by, the fixer told him all about it. "Aren't you worried that the king will find out what you have done to the sword?" asked the disguised king.

"No one will know anything about it," he said. "I can fix anything, and neither the king nor anyone else will be any the wiser."

"You aren't worried at all?" asked the king.

"What's the use of worrying?" said the fixer. "I'm as happy as I've ever been."

The next day, when the king returned to the palace, he summoned the officer of the guard and said, "There is a criminal in the prison who has been sentenced to death. Call the fixer whom you have recruited and order him to cut off the criminal's head."

The king called all his officers to see the execution.

When the fixer was brought before the king, he fell to the ground, asking, "Your Majesty, what can I do for you?"

"I want you to cut off this man's head," said the king, pointing to the criminal.

"But Your Majesty," said the fixer, "I've never killed so much as a fly. I certainly can't kill a man."

"If you want to be a soldier, you must be prepared to kill," said the king.

"But what if the man is innocent?" said the fixer. "Mistakes can be made."

"Not in this case," said the king. "Soldier, do your duty!"

The fixer saw that the king would not be moved. So he raised his eyes to heaven and said, "God, I have always trusted in you. If you want me to kill this man, then so be it. But if you want me to spare him, let the blade of my sword turn to wood."

With that, he drew his sword, and all the officers saw that the blade was indeed made of wood. Everyone gasped, and the king laughed loud and long.

"You are truly a happy man," he said. "You never worry, you leave everything in the hands of God. You shared your food and wine with me when you thought I was a beggar; now I shall share my food and wine with you. I see that happiness cannot be bought, but it can be taught. I shall enjoy each day for what it brings, and learn how to be happy like you."

THE
GEM PRINCE

ONCE THERE WAS a king who did not have any children. As he did not want his kingdom to pass to a stranger, he consulted doctors, but they could not help him.

The king heard that the Jews had inherited the magical secrets of King Solomon, so he issued a decree that they must pray for him to have a child. The Jews of his country searched among their number for one of the thirty-six Just Men who lie hidden in every generation, for the prayers of such a man would surely be granted.

But when they found a Just Man, and asked him if he could help, praising his wisdom, he answered, "I don't know anything at all."

The Jews told the king this, but he insisted that the Just Man be brought to him.

The king told him, "You must realize that I hold the Jews in the palm of my hand. I can crush them with a word. But I do not wish to speak that word. Instead, I ask you nicely, please help me have a child."

And the Just Man told him, "You will have a child."

Later that year, the queen gave birth to a child — a daughter. The princess was very beautiful, and by the time she was four years old she was already renowned for her sharp intelligence and even sharper tongue. There was nothing she liked better than to show off her skill at music. Kings flocked from other lands just to hear her play the harp; and if they didn't applaud loudly when she finished, she would tell them just what she thought of them, each in his own language.

The king admired the princess as much as anyone, but he still yearned for a son to inherit his kingdom. So he decreed that the Jews must pray for him to have a son.

The Jews searched for the Just Man who had helped them last time, but they could not find him, for once he had accomplished his purpose on earth, he departed this life; he had no reason to live on.

They continued searching until they found another of the hidden Just Men. "You must help us, you are so wise," they said.

"I do not know anything," replied the Just Man.

When this was told to the king, he asked for the Just Man to be brought before him, and said to him, "The Jews are in the palm of my hand. . . ."

The Just Man asked him, "Are you willing to do everything I tell you?"

"Yes," answered the king.

"Then you must bring me one of every type of precious gem known to man, for each gem has its own virtue."

"Even if it costs me half my kingdom, I will do it," said the king.

He called for all the gems in his treasury to be brought to him.

The Just Man took these gems and ground them into a powder, which he mixed into a cup of wine. He made the king drink half the potion, and the queen the other half. "You will have a son made entirely of precious gems," he said, "and he will inherit the virtues of each stone. The emeralds will give him wisdom, the sapphires health, and the amethysts courage." And with that, the Just Man went on his way.

In time the queen gave birth to a son, and the king was filled with joy, even though the child was flesh and blood and not made of gems. The son was as handsome as the daughter was beautiful, and as wise as she was clever. By the age of four he was fluent in all languages and could solve all problems. Kings flocked from other lands just to ask him questions.

Now, the arrival of this talented brother made his sister unhappy, for the kings no longer wanted to hear her play her music or listen to her speak in some exotic tongue. The young prince was so charming and good that he got all the attention. Her only consolation was that at least he wasn't made out of gems, as the Just Man had foretold. That made her feel a bit better.

But one day the boy was whittling a piece of wood and cut his finger. When the princess bandaged the wound, she saw a gemstone gleaming beneath the skin. She was so jealous, she felt sick.

She shut herself in her room and refused to eat or drink. Doctors were called, but they could do nothing. Then sorcerers were called. She asked one of them, "Do you know a spell to turn someone into a leper?"

"Yes," he replied.

"Can another sorcerer cancel the spell?"

"Not if the charm used to cast the spell is thrown into water. Then it cannot be undone."

So the princess learned the spell, and cast it on her brother, and threw the charm into the lake so that the spell could never be lifted.

The prince became a leper. He developed sores all over — first on his nose, then his face, then his whole body. Doctors were called, but they could do nothing. Sorcerers were called, but they could not help either. So finally the king issued a decree that the Jews must pray for the boy to get better.

The Jews searched again for the Just Man who had helped them before. They found him on his knees in prayer. He had been praying to God ever since he had told the king that the prince would be made of gems and it seemed his prophecy had not come true. Until his prediction was fulfilled, the Just Man could not leave this life. "What is wrong?" he asked God. "You know that I did not act for fame or reward, but only for Your glory."

The Just Man went to the king and prayed for the sick prince, but to no avail.

Then he prayed again, and learned in his prayers that the prince was under a spell, and that the charm with which the spell had been cast had been thrown into the lake.

He told the king, "The only way to lift such a spell is for the sorcerer who cast it to be thrown into the lake too."

The king replied, "If it will cure my son, you may throw every sorcerer in the kingdom into the lake."

When the princess heard this, she was scared. She ran to the lake, hoping to fish out the charm. But when she reached for it, she fell into the water and drowned.

The king and queen were distraught, but the Just Man said, "Now the prince will get better."

The prince's skin peeled right off and revealed that he was made entirely of gems, as the Just Man had predicted. And he had the virtue and power of each and every precious stone.

THE TREASURE

ONCE THERE WAS a poor man who dreamed night after night of a great treasure buried under a bridge in Vienna. At last he couldn't bear it any longer. "It's no good," he told his wife. "These dreams are tormenting me. I have to go to Vienna and seek the treasure."

When he arrived, he found the bridge with no trouble, but after that he was flummoxed. It was broad daylight, and he didn't dare start digging for the treasure with so many people around. So he just stood on the bridge, wondering what to do.

A soldier passed by and asked him what he was up to. The poor man thought the best thing was to tell the truth, and hope that the soldier would help him find the treasure and share it with him.

But the soldier only laughed. "You Jews and your dreams!" he said. "Why, I myself dreamed only last night of a great treasure buried in the cellar of a poor, tumbledown house in a distant town — but do you think I would be fool enough to go and look for it?"

The soldier told the poor man every detail of his dream, and as he spoke the poor man felt more and more sure that he knew where the treasure was.

It was in the cellar of his very own house.

"Do you really not want to go and find the treasure?" he asked the soldier.

"No," said the soldier scornfully. "There's no treasure. It was just a stupid dream."

"But what if it's real?" asked the poor man.

"If it's real," said the soldier, "then whoever finds the treasure is welcome to it." And he continued on his way.

The poor man went straight home, and as soon as he reached his house, he started to dig up the cellar floor. His wife thought the disappointment of not finding the treasure in Vienna must have driven him mad.

But sure enough, before long he unearthed a wooden casket full of gold coins.

"I had the treasure all along," he told his wife, "but in order to find it, I had to look for it in Vienna."

THE MERCHANT
AND THE POOR MAN

ONCE THERE WAS a rich merchant who had everything money could buy. And nearby there was a poor man who had nothing at all. Their lives couldn't have been more different, except that neither of them had any children.

One night the merchant dreamed a dream. A band of strangers came to his house and started packing up all his possessions. "What are you doing?" he asked. "We're taking everything to the poor man," they replied. And however much the merchant shouted and spluttered at them, they took no notice. They just kept calmly packing his belongings and taking them away until nothing remained in his house but the bare walls. There was nothing he could do about it.

When he woke up, his heart was beating fast and he was drenched with sweat. It took him a moment to realize it was only a dream. "Thank God," he said. "I am still rich." But even so, the dream worried him. He couldn't get it out of his mind.

Before this frightening dream, the merchant used to help the poor man and his wife by giving them a little here, a little there. Now he grew even more concerned for them. But where before he always gave with a cheerful smile, now when he saw them he would grow pale, as if he were afraid. For the dream had seemed so real, he could not help worrying that it meant he would one day lose all his wealth.

One day the poor man's wife called at his house, and he gave her some money. His hand trembled as he stammered, "T-t-t-ake this."

"What is wrong?" she asked. "Are you unwell?"

"No," he said, "but I cannot stop thinking about a terrible dream I had. Strangers came to my house and carried off all my belongings to give to you and your husband, and there was nothing I could do to stop them."

"Was this on the night of the last new moon?" she said.

"Yes. Why do you ask?"

"Because I, too, had a strange dream that night. I dreamed that I was very rich, and that strangers came to my house and packed up all my belongings. When I asked them what they were doing, they said they were taking everything to the poor man. 'What poor man?' I asked. 'You know, the merchant,' they replied. So there's no need to upset yourself about your dream. Everybody has dreams."

But after hearing this, the merchant was even more frightened and anxious than before. It seemed to be fated that he and the poor man should change places. He was terrified.

Shortly after this, the merchant's wife went for an outing in her carriage. She invited several women to join her, and one of them was the poor man's wife.

On the road they met a general and his army who were returning to their own land from the wars. The general, seeing a coach full of women, told his soldiers, "Bring me the prettiest one." And they pulled the poor man's wife from the coach and made her come with them.

The general took the poor man's wife to his home overseas and tried to persuade her to marry him. "Forget your old life," he said. But she refused. She put her trust in God and would not listen to the general. So he locked her up in his house until she changed her mind.

When the merchant's wife and her friends arrived home without her, the poor man was distraught. He threw himself to the floor and wept bitter tears.

The merchant, hearing what had happened, visited the poor man. When he saw him lying on the floor weeping, he said, "Now, now, it's no use carrying on like that."

But the poor man replied, "Some people have wealth, and others have children. All I had was my wife, and now she has been taken from me. So what do I have left?" And he continued to sob as if he had nothing left to live for.

The merchant felt so sorry for the poor man that he forgot all about his own worries. He found out the country where the general lived and went there. And when he came to the general's door he just walked straight in,

right past the guards. He didn't even look at them. Because of that, they thought he had the right to be there.

He found the poor man's wife fast asleep in her room and woke her up. "Come!" he said.

When she saw him, she didn't know what was happening. But he said, "Don't be frightened. Come with me now." So she took his arm, and they walked out of the house as if they had every right to do so. It was only when they had got past the guards that the merchant realized what a mad risk he had run.

"They will soon raise the alarm," he said. "We must hide." Together they took shelter in a tank full of rainwater and stayed there for two days while the soldiers scoured the streets in search of them.

During the two days in the tank, the poor man's wife thought how selfless and brave the merchant had been, and swore an oath that whatever happened she would never forget his kindness. "If, in the future, I can help you, I will give you anything you ask." And she called upon the rainwater to be her witness.

When they judged it safe to leave the tank, they went on their way. But they soon realized that the soldiers were still looking for them, so they took refuge once more, this time in a pool of water. Once again, the poor man's wife took an oath to help the merchant if ever she were in a position to do so, and she called upon the pool to be her witness.

Seven times they took refuge in water to evade the general's men — first in the rainwater tank, then in the pool, then in a spring, a stream, a lake, and a river, and finally in the sea. And each time the poor man's wife swore her oath and called on the waters of their hiding place to be her witness.

Once they reached the sea, the merchant, who had trading connections in every country, was able to find a ship to take them back to their land. There was great joy when he brought the poor man's wife home.

◆　◆　◆

For his goodness, the merchant was rewarded. That year, God granted him the gift of a son.

And for her virtue, the poor man's wife was also rewarded. That year, God granted her the gift of a daughter.

The little girl was extremely beautiful — so much so that when people saw her they mumbled, "May she be spared," and made the sign against the evil eye.

People came from far and wide to marvel at her beauty. They showered her with gifts, and soon the poor man grew rich.

The merchant thought about all this, and he decided that the meaning of his dream must be that his son was destined to marry the poor man's beautiful daughter.

One day, when the poor man's wife paid him a visit, the merchant told her about this idea, and she replied, "I have had the same thought. And if that is what you want, I will go along with you. Have I not sworn that my good fortune will always be yours?"

So the boy and girl were pledged to be married and were sent to school together.

As the girl grew, she became even lovelier. People felt it was worth a long journey just to set eyes on her. Even the lords and ladies came to see her, and because her beauty was so rare, they began to wonder whether she might not make a more suitable wife for one of their sons than the son of a mere merchant.

Still, the son of a nobleman could not marry the daughter of a commoner, however rich he had become. So the lords and ladies arranged that the poor man should enter the service of the king.

He started out as a sergeant, but that didn't last long. Every time a new nobleman decided that he wanted the daughter to marry his son, he would use his influence to advance the poor man's career. So before long, he was a general. And, in fact, the poor man made a very good general. The king sent him off to fight wars, and he always won. So when the king died, the people acclaimed the poor man as king. And the ministers met and agreed to make him king.

Now his success began to go to his head. His rise to power was so swift, he did not see why it should ever stop. Soon all the kings in the world agreed that he should rule over them. They made him emperor of the whole world, and gave him a document saying so in letters of gold.

All this while, the poor man had put off his daughter's suitors because she was already promised to the merchant's son. But now that he was emperor, the poor man was no longer so keen for his daughter to marry the son of a mere merchant. Still, his wife, who was now empress, would not break off the engagement. Although he was emperor of the whole world, he could not overrule his wife, or persuade her to change her mind.

He used his power as emperor to ruin the merchant and reduce him to poverty. An emperor can do that. But still his wife refused to break off their daughter's engagement.

The emperor realized that as long as the merchant's son was alive, he would never be able to arrange a suitable marriage for his daughter. So he trumped up charges against the young man and told the judges to sentence him to death. An emperor can do that. And the young man was condemned to be tied up in a sack and thrown into the sea.

The empress was deeply grieved, but she could

not oppose her husband. All she could do was go to the men whose job it was to throw the merchant's son into the sea. She fell at their feet, and begged them to put some real criminal in his place, and spare the merchant's son, who was innocent and had done nothing wrong. They listened to her plea and cast a murderer into the sea, letting the young man go. He fled the country.

The empress had often told her daughter the story of how the general stole her away, and how the merchant came to rescue her, and how in seven places of concealment she had sworn an oath to help him, and called on the waters of each hiding place to be her witness. So when the young man was imprisoned and condemned to death, the daughter sent him a letter in prison saying that she was still promised to him as his bride. She drew him a map showing the seven places where her mother and his father had hidden, and which were the witnesses to her mother's oath. "Take great care of this letter," she wrote, and she signed it with her name. And he took it with him into exile.

The young man took passage on a ship. A great storm came up, and the ship was wrecked on a desert coast. All the passengers were saved and reached the shore. But as they had been blown far from any shipping route, they had little hope of rescue. They decided to split up, and each go in search of food and water.

The young man walked far from the shore. When he decided to turn back, he could no longer tell which direction the shore was. So he trudged on across the desert.

At last he came to habitable land, with trees and a stream. No one lived there, but there was water to drink and fruit to eat. He had a bow and arrow to defend himself against wild animals and to hunt, and he could reach into the stream with his hand and lift fish from the cool water. Here, he could live.

The emperor thought that the sentence had been carried out, and the merchant's son was dead. Now he was free to arrange a suitable match for his daughter. He began to discuss possible marriages with various kings.

He built a palace for his daughter, and she lived there with the daughters of the nobility as her companions. They entertained themselves by playing musical instruments and telling stories.

The emperor's daughter refused to allow him to arrange a marriage for her, but insisted that all her suitors must come in person and woo her with poetry. She had a special stage constructed, where she made each suitor stand and recite his love poem.

Although they were all the sons of kings, they were not all the sons of poets. Some were clumsy and crude; others were boastful and brash; some were witty and graceful; a few spoke with true passion and feeling. To each one she replied in kind, with a poem of her own. And always at the end she said these words, which no one understood: "But the waters have not blessed you."

Kings and princes came from all over the world seeking her hand in marriage, but all of them received the same reply.

Meanwhile, the merchant's son made his home in the wilderness. For amusement, he fashioned himself a musical instrument from wood, with strings of gut, and sang songs to which he wrote the words himself. And when he felt sad and lonely he took out the letter from the emperor's daughter and remembered everything that had happened to bring him to this desolate spot.

He kept the letter hidden in a tree on which he had carved a special mark. But one day there was a terrible storm, and all the trees were blown down. They lay there smashed and ruined, and he could not tell which was the tree with his mark.

The merchant's son was beside himself with grief. He knew he could not live alone in the wreckage of the forest without the consolation of the letter; he would go mad. So he decided that whatever happened, he must move on. It was more dangerous to stay than to go.

Taking some meat and some fruit, he set off, making marks as he went so that he could find his way back. After a long while the merchant's son reached a village. He asked the people there if they had ever heard of the emperor of the whole world. "Yes," they told him. "The emperor rules over every land. He has a beautiful daughter, but no suitor can win her hand in marriage. She tells them all, 'The waters have not blessed you.' " And the merchant's son remembered how the waters had seven times blessed and protected his father and her mother, and stood witness to her sacred oath, and how the emperor's daughter had drawn him a map of those seven hiding places in the letter he had lost.

He made his way to the king of that land and told him the whole story. "So you see," he finished, "I am the rightful bridegroom of the emperor's daughter, and she will accept no suitor who does not know the secret of the seven hiding places. But I cannot go to claim her, for the emperor would kill me out of hand."

The king was a cunning man, and said, "If you tell me the secret, I will go and claim her and bring her back to you." But the king had no intention of giving up the emperor's daughter, and as soon as he had learned the secret of the hiding places, he banished the merchant's son to a distant land.

The merchant's son was very angry to be treated so shabbily, and he went to the king of his new land and told him the same story. This time he gave the king even more details and urged him to go as quickly as he could to win the emperor's daughter for him. The second king also banished the merchant's son as soon as he had learned the secret.

Once again the merchant's son was furious to be betrayed by a man he had trusted. He went to the king of his new land and told his story once more. This time he even showed the king how to draw the map of the seven hiding places as a final proof. But this king was no more trustworthy than the others, and as soon as he had learned the secret, he banished the merchant's son to a distant land.

Meanwhile the first king had arrived at the palace of the emperor's daughter. He stood on the stage and recited his poem. In it he mentioned all seven places where her mother and the merchant had hidden in water. But he muddled them up so that they were in the wrong order.

Nevertheless the emperor's daughter thought that he must be her bridegroom, grown into a man and returned to claim her. She told herself that he only altered the order of the hiding places in order to make the rhyme work. So she said she would marry him.

There was great rejoicing that the emperor's beautiful daughter had at last found a suitor she would marry. When the second king arrived, he was told not to bother to recite his poem; it was too late. But he insisted and, standing on the stage, he too worked all the seven hiding places into his poem — but this time in the right order.

The emperor's daughter did not know what to think. The first man had seemed to be the right one, but now this second man also knew the signs, and he had not made any mistakes.

When the third king arrived, she was even more confused. For this king not only knew all the hiding places in the right order, he could also draw a map of them, just as she had done in her letter.

She told her three suitors that she would not believe any of them to be the right man until one of them brought her the letter, signed with her own name. But they each had a different excuse for having lost the letter.

Now the merchant's son himself was in despair after all three kings listened to his story, learned his secrets, and then banished him. He decided that his only option was to risk going in person to claim his bride. He begged passage on a ship that took him across the seas to the emperor's castle.

When he stood on the stage, his poem was the most convincing yet. He wove in little incidents from their school days, the tale of how he had hidden and then lost the letter, the story of how he had trusted the three kings, and of course every detail of their parents' escape from the general and the secret of the seven hiding places. And he too was able to draw the map.

By now the emperor's daughter was utterly bewildered. She had thought the first king was him, then the second, then the third. Although her heart told her this was the one, she would not believe it unless he could bring her the letter.

The merchant's son knew that if he stayed to try to convince her, the emperor would have him killed. He realized he must retrace his steps and go back to his home in the wilderness to search for the letter. But when he reached the forest again, one fallen tree looked much like another to him, and however hard he looked, he could not find the hidey-hole where he had left it.

At last, though he still loved the princess with all his heart, he had to admit he might never find the letter. He decided to live out his days in peace and solitude, far from the treachery and heartbreak of the world. So he settled back into his old life, eating the fruit of the trees and drinking water from the stream.

Now on the seas there was a pirate, who heard tell of the emperor's beautiful daughter, and how she had rejected all her suitors and driven so many kings and princes mad with love. He decided to kidnap her and sell her to the highest bidder.

He sailed to the port near her castle, posing as a merchant with goods to sell. To support this pretense he filled his ship with rich merchandise, and also crafted three golden birds, which he kept hidden in a cabin. By means of wires, they could be made to chirp, whistle, and sing for all the world as if they were living creatures.

Many people came to his ship to buy goods, and eventually the princess sent him a note, asking him to bring her a selection of his merchandise. But he replied that it was not his custom to take his goods to the buyer; even the emperor's daughter must come to him.

So the emperor's daughter set off with her guards to visit the ship, taking care first to veil her face so that passersby should not faint in the street when they saw her beauty. She bought a number of items from him, but he said, "These are not my choicest treasures; those are in another cabin." And he pointed to the cabin where the golden birds were.

"I must see those," said the emperor's daughter.

"Very well," said the pirate, "but only you. These are rare works of art, not to be gawped at by just anyone."

So the emperor's daughter went with the pirate into the room with the golden birds, and he locked the door behind them, with the guards on the other side.

The birds were wonderful. They twittered and trilled as beautifully as nightingales as the sun goes down, and the trembling way they balanced on their slender stalks made it almost look as if they were truly flying.

The emperor's daughter was so entranced she did not notice what the pirate was doing. Before she could cry out, he pulled a sack over her head and tied her up. Then he called out to one of his men, who had been hidden behind a panel operating the birds, and dressed him in her clothes, making sure that the veil completely covered his face. When the sailor came out of the cabin, the guards followed him all the way back to the palace, and only realized their mistake when he lifted his veil and they saw his black beard.

The guards rushed back to the pirate's ship, but it had already sailed. They pursued it and eventually caught it, but the pirate was not there, and nor was the emperor's daughter. Knowing that the guards would follow the ship, the pirate had stayed onshore. He and the emperor's daughter hid in a tank filled with rainwater, just as her mother and the merchant had done. "Don't make a noise, if you value your life," he said. "If we are discovered, I am a dead man. I have nothing to lose, and if you make the slightest sound, I will strangle you with my bare hands." Even when she heard the guards go past, the emperor's daughter did not dare call out.

Soon they left the rainwater tank. But whenever the pirate felt he might be in danger, they took refuge again, and in this way they hid in the same kinds of hiding places as her mother and the merchant — a rainwater tank, a pool, a spring, a stream, a lake, a river, and finally the sea. And when they reached the sea, the pirate stole a fishing boat and sailed away with the emperor's daughter, to find a king who would pay to make her his wife. In order that no one would see her beauty and try to take her away from him, he made her wear a sailor's clothes, so that she looked like a man.

As they sailed across the sea, a storm arose and dashed their boat to pieces against the very desert shore where the merchant's son had been ship-wrecked years before.

The emperor's daughter was swept to land and hurried out into the desert to escape the pirate. She could hear him cursing on the shore, shouting, "Come back, or I'll kill you!" She fled as fast as she could.

The pirate tried to track her, but he was soon lost in the desert. He wandered around in circles, unable to find anything to eat or drink, and at last was eaten by wild animals.

The emperor's daughter walked and walked across the desert, and eventually she came to the wilderness where the merchant's son lived. He was amazed to see another person, but since she was dressed like a sailor, and his hair and beard were overgrown, neither recognized the other.

He asked, "How did you get here, sailor?"

"Shipwrecked," she replied.

"Me too," he said.

And so they settled down to live together, neither of them knowing who the other really was.

When the empress heard that her daughter had been abducted by the pirate, she was grief stricken. She wailed that it was all her husband's fault. "You killed the merchant's son, and now you have lost our daughter. What use are your wealth and position now? You have lost my most precious treasure. She was all I had. What do I have left?" And she beat her head against the wall.

The emperor was distraught about the loss of his daughter, but he would not accept that it was his fault. He and his wife argued so bitterly about it that he lost his temper and banished her.

After that, everything started to go wrong for the emperor. The next time he sent his army out to fight a war, they lost. He blamed the general and banished him. But it happened again, and again, until all the generals in the army had been banished.

Then the people banished the emperor and recalled the generals. They asked the empress to come back and be their ruler. Her first act was to ask the ruined merchant and his wife to come and live with her, and share her good fortune.

As for the emperor, he set sail across the sea. A storm arose, which wrecked his ship and cast him away on a desert coast. He walked through the desert until he came to the wilderness where his daughter and the merchant's son were living. He did not recognize them, for his daughter was still disguised as a sailor and many years had passed since he had seen the merchant's son; neither did they recognize this ragged man as the former emperor of the whole world.

"How did you get here?" they asked.

"Shipwrecked," he replied.

"Us too," they said.

And so all three began to live together, none of them knowing who the others really were.

The young man, who had lived there the longest, looked after the others, hunting for food and cutting wood for their fires. Always, more by force of habit than in hope, the young man searched among the fallen trees to find the one where he had hidden the letter years ago.

One day, as they sat around their fire in the evening, the others asked him to tell them his story.

"I am the son of a merchant," he said. "I grew up in wealth and comfort. I lost everything and have ended up in this wilderness; yet I do not complain. The world is full of wickedness and strife, and this is a place of peace and quiet."

"I knew a merchant once," said the emperor. "When I was a poor man, he took pity on me." And then he asked, "Did you ever hear of the emperor of the world?"

"That villain!" said the merchant's son. And he ground his teeth in anger.

"What do you mean?" asked the emperor.

"I am here because of his cruelty and pride," said the young man. And he told them the whole story.

The emperor asked him, "If the emperor were to fall into your hands now, would you take your revenge on him?"

The young man was quiet for a moment. "No," he said, "I would welcome him at my fireside, as I have welcomed you."

The emperor continued, "I have heard that the emperor's beautiful daughter has been abducted, and that he himself has been driven from his throne."

"Then his cruelty and pride have been his own downfall," said the merchant's son. "But I am sorry to hear that his daughter has suffered for it too."

Then the emperor asked again, "If he were to fall into your hands now, would you take your revenge on him?"

"No," said the young man.

So the emperor said, "I am the emperor, and I have fallen into your hands. Do as you see fit."

And the young man embraced him and welcomed him to his fireside.

Now the emperor's daughter heard all this, and she did not know what to do. She did not dare reveal herself to her father and her bridegroom, for the shock might kill them. And besides, she wanted to go home and get married. So she said, "I have heard that the emperor's daughter swore never to marry until her bridegroom brought her the letter she wrote to him while he was in prison. Do you have the letter?"

"No," said the young man. "It is hidden in one of the fallen trees. I look for it every day, but I have never found it."

"We will help you look," she said.

The next day they went with him to chop wood, and the first tree that the emperor's daughter found was the one in which he had concealed the letter. She gave it to him, but he said, "It has come to your hand, so you should keep it. I have long since decided to live out my days in this wilderness. Take the letter, find her, and marry her."

So the emperor's daughter, who was still disguised as a sailor, said, "I will take the letter, woo her, and win her, if you will both come with me and share my good fortune."

At first the young man was reluctant, for he had given up all worldly dreams; and the emperor was reluctant, for he had been banished and would be risking his life to return. But the emperor's daughter said, "You must come with me. All will be well." And they agreed to go with her.

When they came to the shore, a ship was passing, for it had been blown off course. They hailed it, and it carried them back to the land where the empress now ruled.

Still dressed as a sailor, the daughter went to the empress and said that she had information about the fate of her daughter. She told her everything that had happened, finishing, "And then, still dressed as a sailor, your daughter came to see you, to tell you everything that had happened."

And she looked her mother right in the eyes and was recognized.

The empress and her daughter went out into the town square, where the people had gathered to learn the news of the missing girl. "My daughter has returned!" said the empress. And now everybody could see that the sailor was indeed the emperor's daughter.

The merchant's son then stepped forward, and the emperor's daughter gave him back the letter, saying, "I have wooed her, and won her, and she is yours." And all the people cheered.

Then the emperor's daughter said, "My father is also here. We must welcome him home and forgive him."

But when they looked for him, they could not find him. He had merged back into the crowd, once more a poor man among poor men.

So the poor man's daughter and the merchant's son were married. They took over the kingdom and the empire, and ruled over the whole world. Their happiness was complete.

THE TURKEY PRINCE

ONCE THERE WAS a prince who went out of his mind. He thought he was a turkey. He took off all his clothes and crawled under the table, and stayed there all day long, pecking at the crumbs on the floor.

The king sent for the best doctors, but they could do nothing for him. They said he would never get better. The king was grief stricken.

The king held all his councils in the dining room, hoping the prince would become interested in the great questions of the day and join in the discussions. But when the king asked him, "What do you think?", the prince just made gobbling noises and went back to pecking for crumbs.

Nothing seemed to help. Then one day a wise man came and offered to cure the prince.

The wise man did not talk to the prince or dose him with medicine. Instead he took off his own clothes and crawled under the table, pecking at the crumbs, the flabby skin at his neck wobbling like a turkey's wattles.

The prince was so surprised to be joined in this way that he was shocked into speech. "Who are you, and what are you doing?" he asked.

"I could ask the same of you," said the wise man.

"I'm a turkey," said the prince.

"Me too," said the wise man.

So they stayed companionably beneath the table until the prince became used to his new friend. Then the wise man signaled to the servants to bring him two shirts.

"Are you crazy?" asked the prince. "Turkeys don't wear shirts."

"A turkey is still a turkey even if he wears a shirt," said the wise man. So they both put on a shirt.

Then the wise man signalled for the servants to bring him two pairs of pants. "A turkey is still a turkey even if he wears pants," he said.

The wise man continued in this way until they were both fully dressed. Then he signaled again, and the servants brought him two plates of food from the table. "There's no reason to live on crumbs," he said. "A turkey can still be a turkey and eat good food."

When they had eaten, the wise man said, "Why should we turkeys have to crawl about under the table? A turkey is still a turkey if he sits on a chair."

And so, little by little, the wise man coaxed the prince back to the ways of men. And in due course the prince became king, and ruled the land wisely and well.

THE
LOST PRINCESS

ONCE THERE WAS a king who had six sons and one daughter. He loved her the best of all — but one day he lost his temper with her and shouted, "May the Evil One take you!"

The princess went to her room, and in the morning she was gone.

The king was filled with remorse and searched for her high and low. But she was nowhere to be found.

When the king's minister saw how miserable the king was, he said, "Give me a servant, a horse, and some money, and I will find the lost princess."

He traveled up hill and down dale, across the fields and through the forests, until several years had passed. One day, when he had been wandering in circles through the desert, he found a trodden path and decided to take it. *It may lead somewhere,* he thought.

He followed the path a long way, until at last he came to a magnificent fortified castle, with soldiers standing guard outside its great wooden gates. He was afraid the soldiers would not let him in, but he decided to risk it. He asked his servant to look after the horse and walked up to the castle gates. To his surprise, the guard waved him through without even asking his business.

He wandered through the chilly corridors of the castle until he came to a great chamber where a king was holding court. Musicians were playing all kinds of instruments, and the king was standing in front of them with his crown on his head, waving his hands about.

No one bothered the minister, even when he helped himself to food and drink from the tables. So he settled down in a corner to see what would happen next.

The king called for his queen, and some servants went to fetch her. The musicians blew a fanfare on their trumpets when she came into the room. It was the princess!

The princess could feel someone staring at her from the corner of the room. She stole a glimpse and, when she saw who it was, she rose from her throne and went across to him. She touched him on the arm and asked, "Do you know who I am?"

"Yes," he said. "You are the lost princess. I have been searching for you for years. But how did you come to be here?"

"Because of my father's angry words," she replied. "He said, 'May the Evil One take you!', and this is the castle of the Evil One."

The minister told her not to give up hope. "There must be some way to save you," he said.

"There is only one way," answered the princess. "You must find a lonely spot and stay there for a year. For the whole of that year, you must yearn for me. And after I have been in your thoughts for a whole year, you will be able to set me free. But on the last day you must fast, and go without sleep."

The minister went away and did as the princess said. He fixed his mind on the princess and thought of her every minute of every day. On the last day, he denied himself food or sleep, and set out, tired and hungry, for the castle. But on the way he saw a tree laden with luscious apples. Without

thinking, he reached out his hand, plucked one, and took a bite. At once he fell into a deep sleep. His servant shook him, but he could not be roused.

When at last he awoke, he asked, "Where am I?"

His servant told him the whole story. "You have been sleeping here for years," he said. "I have only kept myself alive by eating the apples."

The minister was full of shame. He went back to the castle and told the princess what had happened.

She was filled with sadness. "If you had come, you could have set me free," she said. "But you could not resist temptation. Still, it is difficult to go without food, especially on the very last day, which is the hardest of all."

"If only I had another chance, I would be stronger," said the minister.

"If you wish to try again," she said, "you must spend another year with your thoughts fixed on me. This time you may eat as many apples as you like on the way to set me free, so long as you do not fall asleep. So be careful not to drink any wine, or you will be overtaken by slumber. Remember: Stay awake!"

He went away and did as she said. On the last day, he set out once more for the palace. On the way he passed a spring. "This is strange," he said. "The water in this spring is red and smells almost like wine." He bent down and scooped some of the liquid into his mouth with his hand. At once he fell asleep and could not be woken.

While he was asleep, the princess happened to pass by in her carriage, escorted by a troop of soldiers. When she recognized the minister, she tried to wake him, but he did not stir. Then she began to lament, saying, "After all the years of searching, you could not hold out for one day. You might have set me free, but for the sake of one drink, you have failed me. I am still a captive and cannot escape."

She began to weep. Taking the scarf from her head, she wrote a message on it with her tears and left it lying by him. Then she got back into the carriage and went on her way.

When the minister awoke, he asked, "Where am I?"

His ancient servant told him the whole story. He described how the soldiers had marched past, and he had hidden from them, and how the princess had lamented her fate, and left a message written in tears on her scarf.

So the minister held the scarf up to the light to see what was written there in the princess's tears. "Seek me in the castle of pearl, on top of the golden mountain," it read.

"I must go," said the minister, "and I must go alone." He left his servant and his horse, and set off to look for the princess.

After several years of fruitless searching in the lands of men, he thought, *There is no golden mountain, nor castle of pearl, among the dwellings of men. Therefore I must search in the wilderness.*

As he walked through the wilderness, he met a giant who carried a huge tree as a staff. And the giant asked him, "Who are you?"

"I am a man," he answered.

"I have lived all my life in the wilderness," said the giant, "and I have never seen a man here before. What are you doing?"

"I am looking for the castle of pearl, on top of the golden mountain."

"There is no such place," said the giant.

But the minister insisted. "I know it exists somewhere."

"Stuff and nonsense," said the giant. "But as I am the master of all the beasts, I will call them to me, and see if they know anything about a castle of pearl."

So the giant called all the beasts of the world and asked each of them if they had ever seen the golden mountain in their travels, but none of them had. "It's just a fairy tale," he said. "You are searching for something that does not exist. You should turn back."

But the minister would not be discouraged. "I know it exists somewhere," he said.

So the giant said, "My brother, who lives even deeper in the wilderness, is the master of all the birds. Go to him, and he may be able to help you."

After several years, the minister found the second giant, who also carried a tree. He explained his search, and the giant replied, "There is no such place." However, the minister insisted, so the giant called all the birds of the air and asked each of them if they had ever seen the golden mountain in their flight, but none of them had.

"See," said the giant, "it doesn't exist. You should turn back."

But the minister said, "I know it exists somewhere."

So the giant told him, "Even deeper in the wilderness lives my brother, who is the master of the winds. They blow all over the world, so perhaps they will know."

So the minister went on, and after several years he found the third giant, who also carried a tree. Once more he explained his search, and once more he was told, "There is no such place." But the minister insisted, and so the giant said, "Very well. I will summon the winds."

The giant asked each of the winds in turn, but none of them knew anything about the golden mountain or the castle of pearl. He turned to the minister and said, "You see, it's a fairy tale."

The minister began to weep, but he said through his tears, "I know it exists somewhere."

Just then there arrived one last wind — barely more than a breeze. The giant was angry, saying, "You're late! All the other winds came when I called. Why didn't you?"

The wind answered, "I was busy. I was carrying a princess to a castle of pearl on top of a golden mountain."

The minister was filled with joy. He asked, "What is it like there?"

The wind said, "It is full of things that glitter and shine, but the air above it is filled with sighs and groans."

Then the giant said to the minister, "You have been searching for a long time, but now your trials are over. Take this purse. It will always be full of money." And then he ordered the wind to carry the minister to the golden mountain.

The wind lifted the minister into the air and bore him to the gates of the city in which stood the castle of pearl. Soldiers were standing guard there, and they tried to bar his way, but he reached into the purse and bribed them with silver and gold, and they let him pass into the city.

The minister knew that even now it would be a long, hard task to free the princess. It would need both time and cunning.

And how he managed it, the tale does not tell.

But in the end, he did.

NOTES ON THE STORIES

Rabbi Nahman's stories are regarded by his followers as sacred texts, in which every single word and image is precious. These retellings do not pretend to be word-for-word translations of Nahman's storytelling, such as those of Arnold J. Band or Rabbi Aryeh Kaplan. Instead, while treating the originals with respect, I have hoped to shape a collection of Nahman's tales that will be accessible and enjoyable for a wide general audience.

Rabbi Nahman himself well understood that the same story may need to be told in different ways at different times. Before he told his last story, "The Seven Beggars," he told his followers that he had a story to tell that had only been told once previously, and that was before Solomon's temple was built. "Although the story has already been told once," he said, "it is now totally new. Many things have changed in it since it was last told. For then it was told for that time, and now it is told for this time."

THE PIRATE PRINCESS

This, the second fairy tale that Rabbi Nahman told, is one of his strangest. The story's title (given by Nahman's disciple Rabbi Nathan, not by Nahman himself) is "The King and the Emperor," but as the focus of attention is on the princess, I have followed Howard Schwartz's example in *Elijah's Violin* and renamed it "The Pirate Princess."

Behind all Nahman's fairy tales lies the myth of creation formulated by the great kabbalist Isaac Luria (1534–1572). According to Luria, God originally took up all of space-time. In order to make room for the universe, he contracted himself. This caused a violent cataclysm — a kind of mystical "Big Bang" — in the course of which part of the divine spirit was expelled or exiled from the presence of God. This wandering part of God is called the Shekhinah, and is represented in Nahman's tales by the figure of the princess. It is the role of the Messiah to rescue the Shekhinah and repair the cosmos.

In "The Pirate Princess," the Shekhinah is seen not as the passive captive of Nahman's first tale, "The Lost Princess" (placed last in this book), but as an active shaper of the world. It is the princess who, in the end, rescues the prince, not the other way round. As Arthur Green writes in *Tormented Master,* "She has but one purpose as she goes through the world, a purpose she strives to fulfill with a singlemindedness that may include some cruelty. All she desires is to be reunited with the original intended; the affections of all other suitors are only to be used as stepping-stones along the way."

So much is clear, but much else remains mysterious. To quote Nahman of Cheryn, "The secret of this tale has not yet been interpreted. What may we say of it, especially we who know nothing of hidden things?" This being the case, I have taken the liberty of radically altering the original, from the point at which the princess and her waiting women adopt men's attire.

In the original, they come across another ship which contains a king who, to impress his new bride, climbs to the top of the mast. While he is up there, the princess focuses a reflecting glass on his head and burns his brains. He falls dead into the sea. His ship then pulls alongside that of the princess, hoping there may be a physician aboard. The princess is able to tell them the king has died because his brain has been burned. They make the princess their king and decide to marry her to the widowed queen. The princess commands everyone in the land to attend the wedding, thus attracting her three suitors. The story then proceeds much as it does in my version, except at the end she says to the prince, "Let's go home," rather than staying and ruling the land with him.

To make such alterations in one of Rabbi Nahman's tales is of course to corrupt its hidden kabbalistic meaning — but as not even experts in the kabbalah seem to agree what this meaning is, I was reluctant to leave such a cruel and confusing episode in a story that otherwise has such a clear and attractive narrative line.

I have replaced it with the well-known folktale motif of choosing a new king by means of a "Bird of Happiness," taken here from the story "A Servant When He Reigns" in Dov Noy's *Folktales of Israel*. The same motif occurs in a story of the Uighur people from northwest China, "A Clever Woman," which has many similarities with "The Pirate Princess." In it, a devoted couple is separated when a lustful king kidnaps the woman. She escapes, but is then pestered with attentions from various other men, whom she promises to marry but outwits. One, who is a villain like the pirates in Rabbi Nahman's story, she kills by pouring boiling oil over his bald head; four, who are gamblers, she makes drunk with strong wine. At last she decides to wear men's attire. When the bird alights on her, she is made king. As in Rabbi Nahman's story, her various suitors make their way to her court, and are served as they deserve. When her true husband comes, she marries him and they rule together.

The basic story structure of "The Pirate Princess" is taken from a folktale such as this, a type known to folklorists as "The Abandoned Bride Disguised as a Man." But David G. Roskies, in *A Bridge of Longing*, also points out a connection with a popular Yiddish romance of the nineteenth century, *Mordecai and Esther, a Beautiful and Wondrous Story about a Groom and a Bride*, showing that Rabbi Nahman drew inspiration for his plots from a wide variety of sources, literary as well as oral.

THE FIXER

The story of "The Fixer" is said to have been told by Rabbi Nahman on August 18, 1806, about a month after he told "The Lost Princess." It is therefore one of his earliest tales, among the ones that were most clearly modeled on existing folktales. The archetypal story here is "The Sword That Turned to Wood," a rare folktale type that seems to be particularly common in Jewish tradition.

This tale was not included in the official canon of Nahman's tales, perhaps because it was so obviously based on a traditional story; it was first printed in 1905 by Rabbi Tzvi Dov ben Avraham of Berdichev. There are also some parallels with a more common tale type, "The Luck-Bringing Shirt," in which a discontented king is told he will only be happy when he puts on the shirt of a happy, or lucky, man. He sends his ministers searching far and wide — but the only happy man they find is so poor that he does not possess a shirt!

Rabbi Nahman is known to have told relatively faithful versions of other traditional tales, including "The Master Thief," "The Golden Bird," and "The Treasure at Home" (see "The Treasure" in this volume).

THE GEM PRINCE

Before telling this story, his fifth original fairy tale, Rabbi Nahman said, "I know a tale that contains the entire forty-two letter name of God." Rabbi Aryeh Kaplan suggests that, as the name of Yocheved, the mother of Moses, has the numerical value 42 in the Hebrew alphabet, this means that the prince in the story represents Moses, and the precious gems the Jewish nation. In Exodus 4:6, God momentarily turns Moses into a leper.

As noted in the Introduction, Rabbi Nahman considered himself the spiritual heir to Moses, so no doubt the prince also signifies the storyteller himself, who, like Hans Christian Andersen, puts himself at the center of all his tales. Each of the wise Jews is referred to as a zaddik (righteous man), the term used by the Hasidim for masters such as Rabbi Nahman, and therefore the storyteller must also have seen himself in this role. The reply of each zaddik when asked to help, "I do not know anything at all," is exactly what Rabbi Nahman himself said on the occasion of his last Sabbath teaching in August 1810:

Why do you come to me? I don't know anything at all now. When I teach Torah, there is some reason to travel in order to be with me. But why have you come now? I don't know anything now; I'm just a simple person.

The story also contains several hints that these zaddikim relate to the folklore of the Lamed Vav, or thirty-six Just Men, who exist in secret in every generation. It is because of these Just Men that the world continues to exist.

As Rabbi Nahman believed he shared a soul with Moses and other great religious leaders, he may have regarded himself as one of the Lamed Vav.

The birth of the princess, when the king really wanted a son, shows, in true fairy tale style, how one must be careful what one wishes for: He asked for "a child," not specifically for a son. Interestingly, the girl is never referred to as a princess, but instead as "the queen's daughter," suggesting that she is somehow not truly the king's child.

THE TREASURE

This little tale was told by Rabbi Nahman as a parable about the need to travel to the zaddik in order to learn how to uncover one's innate spiritual wealth. However, this meaning was simply superimposed on a preexisting folktale, told in many cultures, known to folklorists as "The Treasure at Home."

A well-known English example, in which the treasure is simply material treasure rather than spiritual enlightenment, is the story of "The Pedlar of Swaffham." The tale can also be found in the *Arabian Nights* as well as in the folklore of Northern and Eastern Europe. In Jewish tradition, there are parallels to this story in the Talmud and the Midrash, as well as in orally transmitted folktales.

Rabbi Nahman was not the only Hasidic master to adapt this tale to his teachings; his contemporary Simha-Bunam of Pshiskhe told a longer version, with the moral that "the treasure, the one that is yours, is to be found only in yourself, and nowhere else."

THE MERCHANT
AND THE POOR MAN

This tale is often interpreted as a highly wrought allegory, replete with hidden spiritual meanings. In his edition of Rabbi Nahman's tales, Arnold Band describes it as "a remarkable psychological study of the agonies of the messiah [the merchant's son] confronted with constant frustration in his attempt to bring the final redemption." But it is also a romance, in which two lovers, destined for each other, finally achieve happiness after many troubles and adventures.

Almost every element of the story can be paralleled in a folktale. For instance, the incident where the emperor's daughter is lured onto the ship by the pirate pretending to be a merchant is simply a twist on a favorite folktale motif; in a Romanian story, "The Girl Who Pretended to Be a Boy," in Andrew Lang's *The Violet Fairy Book,* a princess disguised as a man steals away a golden-haired beauty by precisely the same trick.

The core story draws on two fairy tale types, both well known in Eastern Europe: "The Rescued Princess," in which the hero ransoms a princess from slavery, is thrown overboard on the journey home, and then rescued and brought before the princess to prove his identity by recounting his life story; and "The Forsaken Fiancée," in which an abandoned girl disguises herself as a man.

Nahman strips these tale types down to their component parts and then deftly reassembles them in a completely new arrangement, turning the young man and woman at the center of the traditional tales into emblems of the Messiah and the Shekhinah. He reinforces this kabbalistic interpretation by the imagery of the seven types of water, which represent, among other things, the seven watering places in the desert mentioned in the Biblical book of Exodus. The creative freedom with which Nahman remodels his source material produces a story that is completely new and original yet has deep roots in tradition.

THE
TURKEY PRINCE

This little fable, one of the most popular of all of Rabbi Nahman's stories, addresses one of his most private concerns: the need to find a balancing point between madness and sanity.

Nahman wrestled with depressive illness all his life, and said, "Depression can cause a man to forget his name." For this reason he valued the gift of laughter, which he felt came from the part of mankind that is closest to God. In his biography of Nahman, *Tormented Master*, Arthur Green points out how the wise man in this story "has exactly the role which Nahman sought to play among his disciples: he is doctor of souls." But Nahman is not only the wise man; he is also the prince; his wisdom was won from suffering.

Rabbi Nathan, Rabbi Nahman's closest disciple, wrote, "The whole world is mad and so am I; except that I had the good fortune of seeing one lucid being." This "one lucid being" was Rabbi Nahman, and his lucidity is perhaps not so much the absence of madness as the acceptance of it. Once when he was contemplating giving up his teaching, Nahman said, "I shall take my wife and go far away, and from the sidelines I shall observe people and laugh about the things they do."

Rabbi Nahman warned his disciples, "The world will consider you a lunatic if you abandon all worldliness in your quest for the Godly." One of his short parables concerns a king who reads in the stars that whoever eats that year's grain will go mad. He consults his prime minister, who tells him, "There is enough grain left from last year that neither you nor I will have to eat this year's crop. We will both be safe."

"But what about the others?" the king asks. "They will all go mad. If only we two stay sane, the others will think that it is we who are mad. As there is not enough good grain for all, we too must eat this year's tainted grain, and go mad with the rest. But we will put a mark on our foreheads. Then, when we look at each other we shall remember, 'We are mad.'"

This tale is closely paralleled by a Sufi story, "When the Waters Were Changed," in Idries Shah's *Tales of the Dervishes.* In this, a whole village drinks from a well that drives them mad, except one man who has a supply of pure water. But he is so lonely and unhappy at being regarded by the others as the mad one that he too drinks the tainted water, and is hailed by the others as a madman miraculously healed.

Many links can be drawn between Nahman's teaching and Sufi thought, so it is no surprise that one of his most personal stories should so closely echo a Sufi tale. The "crazy wisdom" of such a story can be interpreted in many ways, but it seems that for Rabbi Nahman, one path to redemption in this world of illusion is to embrace our irrational selves, in the full understanding that "we are mad."

THE LOST PRINCESS

"The Lost Princess" was the first fairy tale composed by Rabbi Nahman. He said of it, "I told this story on the way, and everyone who heard it had thoughts of repentance."

In this story, the king at the beginning symbolizes God, while the princess is the Shekhinah — the representation of God's divine presence in the world. To explain the king's temporary rejection of the princess, Rabbi Adin Steinsaltz quotes Isaiah 54:7, "For a small moment have I forsaken thee; but with great compassion will I gather thee."

The minister, who may be seen as either Rabbi Nahman himself, as the Messiah, or as Everyman, ultimately symbolizes the people of Israel in his quest to rescue the princess from the clutches of the Evil One, to restore and redeem her. His is a spiritual quest, and that is why he must undergo spiritual tests set by the princess. In failing these tests, he repeats first the fall of Adam (by eating the apple) and then that of Noah (by drinking the wine).

This explanation, which could be extended and deepened until it is much longer than the tale itself, is perhaps of more interest to Hasidic scholars than to readers drawn by the story's fairy tale qualities. But it is important to know that such a precise inner meaning can be elucidated, because this explains what otherwise must be a mystery — why the story ends so abruptly. Our longing for closure and completion is stirred up and then deliberately thwarted.

In any ordinary fairy tale, we would expect the minister to free the princess, restore her to her contrite father, and perhaps even win her hand in marriage. In his version in *Elijah's Violin and Other Jewish Folktales,* Howard Schwartz supplies such an ending, though without the marriage. But good as Schwartz's completed tale is, it obscures Rabbi Nahman's central point, which is that the final rescue, the redemption of the Shekhinah, still lies in the balance.

The tale's final assertion that the minister *did* free the princess is an act of faith in the future rather than a record of something that is over and done with. The thoughts of repentance with which the story filled its first hearers were, for Nahman, the start of the process of redemption by which the tale's inner meaning could be fulfilled. As Nahman said of the similar missing ending of his last tale, "The Seven Beggars," "We will not be worthy to hear it until the Messiah comes."

In this first tale, Rabbi Nahman stayed closer to the models of the traditional fairy tale than he did in later stories. Even such striking details as the master of the beasts who uses a tree for a staff come from folk tradition; for instance, in the Ukrainian folktale "Ivanko, Tsar of the Beasts," Ivanko first demonstrates his strength by pulling up a tree by the roots. "The Lost Princess" can also be compared to two tale types that were part of both Ukrainian and the wider Indo-European folktale tradition: "The Quest for a Vanished Princess" and "The Accursed Daughter." In the former, the hero rescues a princess who has been imprisoned in the underworld by a monster; in the latter, a man seeks to marry a girl who has been carried off by the devil because of her mother's careless words. But neither of these widespread folktales has the mystical charge of Rabbi Nahman's extraordinary tale. Nor would any traditional storyteller dare to frustrate his audience as Nahman does by bringing the tale to a close before its natural ending.

Nahman said, "Man is a miniature world." In an unforgettable image in his long and complex final tale, "The Seven Beggars," the heart of the world is shaped like a man, crying out in anguish. By dangling before us the promise that this damaged world will one day be redeemed and perfected, bringing both the story of "The Lost Princess" and time itself to an end, Nahman hopes to assuage that anguish and replace it with joy.

FURTHER READING

RABBI NAHMAN

Green, Arthur. *Tormented Master: The Life and Spiritual Quest of Rabbi Nahman of Bratslav.* Woodstock, Vermont: Jewish Lights Publishing, 1992.

Nahman ben Simhah of Bratslav. *Nahman of Bratslav: The Tales.* Translation, Introduction, and Commentaries by Arnold J. Band. New York: Paulist Press, 1978.

—. *Rabbi Nachman's Stories.* Translated with notes based on Breslover works by Rabbi Aryeh Kaplan. Jerusalem: Breslov Research Institute, 1983.

—. *The Tales of Rabbi Nachman of Bratslav.* Retold with commentary by Adin Steinsaltz. Northvale, New Jersey: Jason Aronson, Inc., 1993.

—. *The Empty Chair: Finding Hope and Joy.* Adapted by Moshe Mykoff and the Breslov Research Institute. Woodstock, Vermont: Jewish Lights Publishing, 1994.

Nathan of Nemerov. *Rabbi Nachman's Wisdom.* Translated and annotated by Rabbi Aryeh Kaplan. Edited by Rabbi Zvi Aryeh Rosenfeld. Jerusalem: The Breslov Research Institute, 1973.

Wiskind-Elper, Ora. *Tradition and Fantasy in the Tales of Reb Nahman of Bratslav.* Albany: State University of New York Press, 1998.

JEWISH MYSTICISM AND FOLKLORE

Bin Gorion, Micha Joseph. *Mimekor Yisrael: Selected Classical Jewish Folktales.* Edited by Emanuel bin Gorion. Translated by I. M. Lask. Bloomington and Indianapolis: Indiana University Press, 1990.

Buber, Martin. *Tales of the Hasidim.* New York: Schocken Books, 1991.

Cooper, David A. *God Is a Verb: Kabbalah and the Practice of Mystical Judaism.* New York: Riverhead Books, 1997.

Gaster, Moses. *The Exempla of the Rabbis.* London and Leipzig: Asia Publication Co., 1924. Reprinted, New York: KTAV, 1968.

—. *Ma'aseh Book: Book of Jewish Tales and Legends.* Philadelphia: Jewish Publication Society of America, 1934.

Goldstein, David, and Joseph Dan. *Studies in East European Jewish Mysticism and Hasidism.* Portland, Oregon, and London: Vallentine Mitchell & Co., Ltd., 1997 (The Littmann Library of Jewish Civilization).

Mintz, Jerome R. *Legends of the Hasidim.* Northvale, New Jersey: Jason Aronson, Inc., 1995.

Newman, Louis I., and Samuel Spitz. *The Talmudic Anthology: Tales and Teachings of the Rabbis.* West Orange, New Jersey: Behrman House, Inc., 1945.

Noy, Dov. *Folktales of Israel.* Chicago: The University of Chicago Press, 1963.

Rabinowicz, Tzvi. *The Prince Who Turned into a Rooster: One Hundred Tales from Hasidic Tradition.* Northvale, New Jersey: Jason Aronson, Inc., 1993.

Rapoport-Albert, Ada. *Hasidism Reappraised.* Portland, Oregon, and London: Vallentine Mitchell & Co., Ltd., 1997 (The Littmann Library of Jewish Civilization).

Roskies, David G. *A Bridge of Longing: The Lost Art of Yiddish Storytelling.* Cambridge, Massachusetts: Harvard University Press, 1995.

Sadeh, Pinhas. *Jewish Folktales.* New York: Anchor Books, 1989.

Schwartz, Howard. *Elijah's Violin and Other Jewish Folktales.* New York: Harper & Row, 1983.

—. *Miriam's Tambourine: Jewish Folktales from Around the World.* Oxford and New York: Oxford University Press, 1988.

—. *Adam's Soul: The Collected Tales of Howard Schwartz.* Northvale, New Jersey: Jason Aronson, Inc., 1992.

Weinreich, Beatrice Silverman, and Leonard Wolf. *Yiddish Folktales.* New York: Pantheon Books, 1988.

Wiesel, Elie. *Souls on Fire and Somewhere a Master.* Harmondsworth: Penguin Books, 1984.

Wineman, Aryeh. *Mystic Tales from the Zohar.* Princeton, New Jersey: Princeton University Press, 1998.

GENERAL FOLKLORE

Aarne, Antti. *The Types of the Folktale: A Classification and Bibliography.* Translated and enlarged by Stith Thompson. Helsinki: Suomalainen Tiedeakatemia, 1981 (Folklore Fellows Communications no. 3, 2nd revision).

Afanas'ev, Aleksandr. *Russian Fairy Tales.* Translated by Norbert Guterman. New York: Pantheon Books, 1945.

Ashliman, D. L. *A Guide to Folktales in the English Language: Based on the Aarne-Thompson Classification System.* New York, Westport, Connecticut, London: Greenwood Press, 1987.

Boyko, Volodomir. *Ukrainian Folk Tales.* Translated by Irina Zheleznova. Kiev: Dnipro Publishers, 1981.

He, Liyi. *The Spring of Butterflies and Other Folktales of China's Minority Peoples.* Edited by Neil Philip. New York: Lothrop, Lee & Shepard Books, 1986.

Lang, Andrew. *The Violet Fairy Book.* London, New York, and Bombay: Longmans, Green, and Co., 1901.

Lüthi, Max. *The Fairytale as Art Form and Portrait of Man.* Translated by John Erickson. Bloomington: Indiana University Press, 1984.

—. *The European Folktale: Form and Nature.* Translated by John D. Niles. Bloomington & Indianapolis: Indiana University Press, 1986.

Shah, Idries. *Tales of the Dervishes: Teaching-Stories of the Sufi Masters over the Past Thousand Years.* London: Jonathan Cape, 1967.

Thompson, Stith. *The Folktale.* Berkeley, Los Angeles, London: University of California Press, 1977.